Grandpa lived in the mountains.

It was a long way from Josh.

So Grandpa sent letters to Josh.

Josh sent a letter to Grandpa.

Letters
from
Grandpa

by Jill Atkins and Lisa Williams

FRANKLIN WATTS
LONDON • SYDNEY

Josh lived in the town.

It was a long way from Grandpa.

So Josh sent letters to Grandpa.

The letter made Grandpa
very happy.

Grandpa sent a letter to Josh.

The letter made Josh very happy.

"Grandpa is coming to stay,"

he shouted.

Then Mum got a letter
from Grandpa.

"Oh no!" cried Josh.

"Grandpa is in hospital.
We must go and see him."

"Yes," said Mum.
"We will go today."

Josh packed his bag
and they set off.
They went in a taxi ...

on a train ...

and on a bus.

At the hospital,

Josh ran to see Grandpa.

Grandpa gave Josh a big hug.

"I am glad to see you," he said.

The doctor came to see Grandpa. "You can go home now," she said. "But you need someone to look after you."

"I can look after Grandpa," said Josh.

Josh packed Grandpa's bag
and they set off.
They went on a bus ...

on a train ...

and in a taxi.

"Grandpa can live with us.
We will look after him,"
said Mum.

"We can still send letters,"
said Grandpa.

"And cards, too!" said Josh.

Story trail

Start

Start at the beginning of the story trail. Ask your child to retell the story in their own words, pointing to each picture in turn to recall the sequence of events.

Independent Reading

This series is designed to provide an opportunity for your child to read on their own. These notes are written for you to help your child choose a book and to read it independently.

In school, your child's teacher will often be using reading books which have been banded to support the process of learning to read. Use the book band colour your child is reading in school to help you make a good choice. *Letters from Grandpa* is a good choice for children reading at Green Band in their classroom to read independently.

The aim of independent reading is to read this book with ease, so that your child enjoys the story and relates it to their own experiences.

About the book

Josh and Grandpa live a long way from each other. So they exchange letters. When Grandpa has to go into hospital, Josh and his mum visit. Then Grandpa come homes to live with them. They will still be able to send letters, though!

Before reading

Help your child to learn how to make good choices by asking: "Why did you choose this book? Why do you think you will enjoy it?" Look at the cover together and ask: "What do you think the story will be about?" Support your child to think of what they already know about the story context. Read the title aloud and ask: "The boy in the story gets letters from Grandpa. Do you think he might send some too?" Remind your child that they can try to sound out the letters to make a word if they get stuck.

Decide together whether your child will read the story independently or read it aloud to you.

During reading

If reading aloud, support your child if they hesitate or ask for help by telling the word. Remind your child of what they know and what they can do independently.

If reading to themselves, remind your child that they can come and ask for your help if stuck.

After reading

Support comprehension by asking your child to tell you about the story. Use the story trail to encourage your child to retell the story in the right sequence, in their own words.

Help your child think about the messages in the book that go beyond the story and ask: "Do you think Josh is glad that his grandpa has come to live with him? Why/why not?"

Give your child a chance to respond to the story: "Did you have a favourite part? Would you like to write letters to someone? Who? What sort of things would you write about?"

Extending learning

Help your child understand the story structure by using the same sentence patterning and adding different elements. "Let's make up a new story about Josh sending letters and arranging to meet someone. Josh could be writing to a friend. What will he write about and how will he travel to meet his friend? Will he go in car, or perhaps an aeroplane?"

In the classroom, your child's teacher may be teaching polysyllabic words (words with more than one syllable).

There are many in this book that you could look at with your child: Grand/pa, happ/y, hos/pit/al.

Franklin Watts
First published in Great Britain in 2017
by The Watts Publishing Group

Copyright © The Watts Publishing Group 2017

Series Editors: Jackie Hamley and Melanie Palmer
Series Advisors: Dr Sue Bodman and Glen Franklin
Series Designer: Peter Scoulding

A CIP catalogue record for this book is
available from the British Library.

ISBN 978 1 4451 5449 7 (hbk)
ISBN 978 1 4451 5450 3 (pbk)
ISBN 978 1 4451 6098 6 (library ebook)

Printed in China

Franklin Watts
An imprint of
Hachette Children's Group
Part of The Watts Publishing Group
Carmelite House
50 Victoria Embankment
London EC4Y 0DZ

An Hachette UK Company
www.hachette.co.uk

www.franklinwatts.co.uk